Seen and not Heard

Katie May Green

In a big old house, up creaky stairs,
in a silent little nursery full of dolls
and teddy bears, you'll find the children
of Shiverhawk Hall.

They're children in pictures on the wall
— seen and not heard...

For Mum, Dad and Al
and for Eva ~ with love

First published 2014 by Walker Books Ltd
87 Vauxhall Walk, London SE11 5HJ

This edition published 2015

10 9 8 7 6 5 4 3 2 1

© 2014 Katie May Green

The right of Katie May Green to be identified as author/illustrator of this work has
been asserted by her in accordance with the Copyright, Designs and Patents Act 1988

This book has been typeset in Polipilus MT

Printed in China

British Library Cataloguing in Publication Data:
a catalogue record for this book is available from the British Library

ISBN 978-1-4063-6099-8

www.walker.co.uk

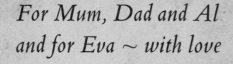
WALKER BOOKS
AND SUBSIDIARIES
LONDON · BOSTON · SYDNEY · AUCKLAND

LILY PINKSWEET

PERCY PINKSWEET

Prudence, Peter and Pearl Plumsey

BILLY FITZBILLIAN III

Lila and Vila De Villechild

LILY PINKSWEET

Prudence, Peter and Pearl Plumsey

BILLY FITZBILLIAN III

Don't they look so sweet and good,
so well behaved,
like children should?

There's little Lily Pinksweet,
a dainty delight,

the Plumseys so grown-up,
their manners so polite.

Billy Fitzbillian is the cleverest boy,

Percy is the kindest,
he'll share any toy.

And as for those twins,
the De Villechild girls, they are ...

PERCY PINKSWEET

Lila and Vila De Villechild

But how do they feel behind their
picture frames when their frocks tickle
and their collars prickle and their noses
itch and they mustn't scratch?
How can they stay so still
and good, sweet little children,
just as they should?

Well, when the night is whispering
and the moon is high,
when there's no one to see them,
when there's no one to spy,
carefully they creep out of the quiet...

LILY PINKSWEET

PERCY PINKSWEET

BILLY FITZBILLIAN III

Lila and Vila De Villechil

The Shiverhawk children ...

all run RIOT!

They race down the hallway, giggling with glee!
"I'll be the leader," says Lily. "Follow me!"
"Midnight feast!" says Percy.
"Ooh, goody, goody, goody!"

And they gallop to the kitchen, shrieking,

"Yippeeeeeeeeeeeee!"

Starting with pudding
is Percy's favourite way to dine.
"Get your paws off
my trifle," he says.
"It's MINE!"

Catching cakes in her
mouth is Lily's best trick.
Sticky ringlets,
jammy ribbons,
fizzy tummy,
"I feel sick."

The Plumseys leave
the pantry,
carrying pots of
treacly goo.
The others hop
from foot to foot:
it's time for
something new.

"Come on,
let's get painting!"
the boys and girls cry.
"That's the way to
do it!" says Billy.
"Dip, slick, a lick,
then dry!"

The fun spins onwards,
upwards, faster,
louder, higher!
Breathless bouncers
whirl and hoot.
Happy hearts
flip and fly!

And then...

Pillows burst ...

and giddy laughter softens into silence,

floating,

fluttering

in the air.

"The moon is getting tired," says Lily.
"Let's get back before the sun!"

And hearing Lily's warning words ...
the children start to run.

They race along the hallway and run up the creaky stairs,
back into their nursery, to their dolls and teddy bears.

•LILY PINKSWEET•

•BILLY FITZBILLIAN III•

PERCY PINKSWEET

Lila and Vila De Villechild

"Oh no!" says Lily Pinksweet,
as she climbs into her frame.
For she sees that Percy's missing,
and must look for him again.
"Come on, Percy, hurry!
You're running out of time!"

And just as the sun creeps in
the room ...

they're all back.

They stay still and sweet and good,
just like children should.

Seen and not heard.